Night Before Christmas

Sue Carabine

Illustrations by
Shauna Mooney Kawasaki

GIBBS·SMITH
PUBLISHER

SALT LAKE CITY

04 03 02   10 9 8

Copyright © 1996 Gibbs Smith, Publisher

Printed in China

Published by
Gibbs Smith, Publisher
P.O. Box 667
Layton, Utah 84041

ISBN 0-87905-764-5
ISBN 1-58685-127-6/GIFT

'Twas the night
before Christmas
when at the North Pole,
St. Nicholas was ready to
perform his great role.

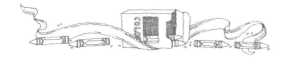

His outfit was striking,
all clean and well pressed,
from the fur on his hat
to the trim on his vest.

Dasher and Dancer
and the rest of the crew
were getting so restless
awaiting their cue.

The bells on their reins just
shimmered and glowed;
their coats shone with
luster, as they strained
at the load.

"I think we're all ready,"
a deep voice announced,
then Santa jumped into
the sleigh
with a bounce.

"The list, fetch the list,
my cheery young elf,
I need to count toys and
make sure of myself."

The elf stared at Santa,
his face looked quite blank.
"The list," he said softly,
and his heart about sank.

"Why, you have it already,
I'm sure that you do.
Look there in your sack,
it's just hidden from view."

"Ho, ho, ho," said St. Nick,
"this is no time for tricks.
I must get a move on or
we'll be in a fix.

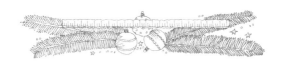

A new list my computer
can readily print.
Run along, little elf,
or better yet, sprint."

The elf stood there trembling,
his hopes all but dashed,
as he gently told Santa
the hard drive
had crashed.

"No, no, no," boomed out
St. Nick, "that list
was checked twice.
It must print
or we won't know
who's naughty or nice."

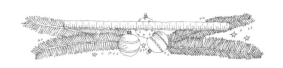

Mrs. Claus stood there
smiling and patting
young Prancer,
"Calm down,
my dear husband,
'cause I have the answer.

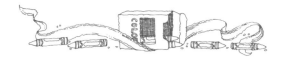

"Those wonderful people
who mold the world's future
can solve any problems —
I believe they're called
'Teacher.'

I'll get the word to them
from East Coast to West,
they've seen all the kids
at their worst
and their best.

"Just visit the teachers
before you proceed
to the homes of the
children who expect you
this eve."

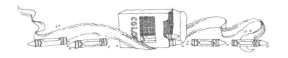

So Santa Claus, chuckling,
sped on his way,
breaking all records
while guiding the sleigh.

To the first teacher's home
he went with great haste,
and she told him these
secrets with no time
to waste.

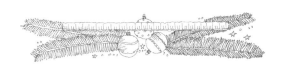

Mrs. Giles in third grade
almost started to yell
when relating
to Santa
of Tom's Show & Tell.

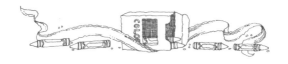

He'd brought a small box
with a wrapper beneath,
which, when he uncovered,
showed Grandma's
false teeth!

"But that's fine, St. Nick,"
she said with a smile,
"the children stopped
giggling after a while,

And Tom is a good boy,
he does well on his tests.
Please make sure you leave
him the gifts he requests."

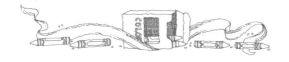

So the Jolly Old Elf
went fast on his way,
learning of kids from what
teachers would say.

He came to a village
that sparkled with snow
Where the faces of children
in sleep had a glow.

Mrs. Jeffers was waiting
to tell him of Jane,
who was there
when it happened
but wasn't to blame.

The plug just blew up,
made a hole
in the wall.
No one was hurt,
not Jane's fault at all.

"She has always
loved science
and told her instructor
that from Santa she
wanted a super conductor.

"So please grant her wish,
for in you she believes,
and a Nobel Prize someday
she just might receive."

Santa laughed loudly
and nodded his head,
trying to remember
all that was said.

He enjoyed spending time
with these teachers so dear;
the love that they had for
their kids was quite clear.

The next town he came to
was filled with such light,
he just couldn't wait to fill
stockings that night.

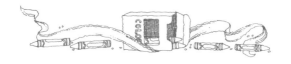

But first St. Nick knew
of a teacher he'd meet
who would give him some
facts till his list
was complete.

This time a twinkle
appeared in the eye
of the teacher
who told him
who made the girls cry.

At five years of age,
Billy never would miss
any chance that he had
to give each girl a kiss!

"But, my dear Santa Claus,
don't let that deter you
from giving to Bill any gift
that you want to.

For, you see, Bill will never
turn someone away
when his help is needed
anytime of the day."

Jolly Old St. Nick was
just about done.
He just couldn't think
when he'd had
so much fun.

Maybe the list
would go missing
next year
and more tales of his kids
from the teachers he'd hear.

Mr. Cox, the last teacher
to give a report,
looked like Santa himself,
was the round, jolly sort.

He said that the children
in their little town
were the best—
very best—
that could ever be found.

He chortled with Santa
and tried to recall
an occasion where
someone was sent
to the hall,

And then he remembered
a few months ago
the problem he'd had
with his sweet little Flo.

He was teaching the kids
about sharp notes and flat,
when down on a big
whoopee cushion he sat!

The children were howling
when Mr. Cox said,
"I expect a confession,
or I shall see red."

Little Flo pleaded guilty
to the terrible crime
by raising her hand
in the quick
nick of time.

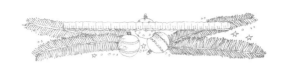

"So Santa, she's honest.
I don't blame her a bit;
to stop collapsing from
laughter was the
hardest thing yet!"

When Santa
had finished
delivering the toys,
he knew not to worry
about his girls and boys.

They were all being taught
by teachers who care,
although life
for these teachers
was sometimes unfair.

Their skill and their wisdom
helped him save the day.
Now Christmas was here,
he could go on his way.

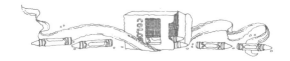

Then he called as his reindeer
flew up with no fuss,
"Merry Christmas,
dear teachers,
you all get an A+."